Pinky and Rex

Other Avon Camelot Books by
James Howe

The Celery Stalks at Midnight • Creepy-Crawly Birthday
The Fright Before Christmas • Hot Fudge • Howliday Inn
Morgan's Zoo • A Night Without Stars • Nighty-Nightmare
Pinky and Rex Get Married • Pinky and Rex Go to Camp
Pinky and Rex and the Mean Old Witch
Pinky and Rex and the Spelling Bee
Rabbit-Cadabra!
Scared Silly

SEBASTIAN BARTH *Mysteries*
Dew Drop Dead • Eat Your Poison, Dear
Stage Fright • What Eric Knew

Avon Camelot Books by
Deborah and James Howe

Bunnicula: A Rabbit-Tale of Mystery

JAMES HOWE is the author of numerous popular books for children, including *The Fright Before Christmas* and *Scared Silly*, and other books about Bunnicula, the vampire rabbit, and his friends, Harold, Chester, and Howie.

The Pinky and Rex books were inspired in part by a child's question about the author's favorite color (he was wearing a pink shirt that day) and by his friendship when he was seven with a girl very much like Rex.

Mr. Howe lives in Hastings-on-Hudson, New York, with his wife, Betsy Imershein, and their daughter, Zoe.

MELISSA SWEET has studied art at the Kansas City Art Institute and currently works as a greeting card illustrator and maker of one-of-a-kind, handmade collector's books. With the Pinky and Rex series, she now enters the world of children's book illustration. Ms. Sweet lives in Boston, Massachusetts, with her husband.

Pinky and Rex

JAMES HOWE

Illustrated by Melissa Sweet

AN AVON CAMELOT BOOK

AVON BOOKS
A division of
The Hearst Corporation
1350 Avenue of the Americas
New York, New York 10019

Text copyright © 1990 by James Howe
Cover and text illustrations copyright © 1990 by Melissa Sweet
Published by arrangement with Atheneum Publishers, an imprint of Macmillan Publishing Company
Library of Congress Catalog Card Number: 89-30786
ISBN: 0-380-71190-7
RL: 2.3

First Avon Camelot Printing: October 1991

CAMELOT TRADEMARK REG. U.S. PAT. OFF. AND IN OTHER COUNTRIES, MARCA REGISTRADA, HECHO EN U.S.A.

Printed in the U.S.A.

DON   10   9   8   7   6   5   4   3

To my niece, Deborah

—J. H.

To Sandy and Max

—M. S.

Contents

Chapter 1
Pinky and Rex
Get Dressed

"Wake up, Pinky!"

Pinky's eyes popped open. His little sister, Amanda, was jumping up and down on his bed. "Wake up, wake up!" she cried.

"I am awake," said Pinky. "Stop jumping on my bed!"

1

"We're going to the museum!" Amanda shouted. She did not stop jumping. "We're going to see the dinosaurs! Hurry up, Pinky, get dressed."

Pinky got out of bed and ran to
the window. "Rex!" he called out.
"Rex!" he called again.

"Hi, Pinky!" Rex called back
from a window in the house across
the street. "I can't decide what to
wear to the museum today. Should I

wear my tyrannosaurus T-shirt or my
stegosaurus sweatshirt?"

"Wear your tyrannosaurus T-shirt,"
Pinky shouted. "It's too hot for a
sweatshirt. What do you think *I*
should wear—my shirt with pink and
white stripes or my shirt with pink
and blue checks?"

"I like the shirt with pink and blue
checks," said Rex. "It's my favorite."

4

"Mine, too," Pinky said. He had never thought that the shirt with pink and blue checks was his favorite. But now that he knew it was Rex's favorite, it was his, too.

"See you later," Pinky shouted.

"See you later," shouted Rex.

"What should *I* wear to the museum today?" Amanda asked her brother.

"Who cares?" said Pinky. And he went to brush his teeth.

Chapter 2
Too Many Animals

When he came back, Amanda was counting his stuffed animals.

"You have *too* many of these things," she said. "You should give me some."

"You say that every morning," said Pinky. "Besides, they're not things, they're my animals."

7

"But you *should*," Amanda insisted. "I have only thirteen animals and you have twenty-seven!"

"When did you learn to count that high?" Pinky asked, because he knew that she was right. He did have twenty-seven animals. And every morning, after he had gotten dressed and after Amanda had told him he had *too* many animals, he said goodbye to them. Each and every one.

He said goodbye to his frog. He said goodbye to his bear. He said goodbye to his kangaroo.

He said goodbye to his elephant, his giraffe, his three cats, his four dogs, his five rabbits, his alligator, his lion, and his tiger.

He said goodbye to his monkey.

9

He said goodbye to his mouse and
his moose and his mole.

   Some animals he hugged
because they were little and needed
to be hugged. Some he patted
because they didn't care to be
hugged first thing in the morning.
And some, like his spider and his

porcupine, he didn't touch at all because they didn't care to be hugged ever.

He always saved his pig for last. Pretzel, named for his curly tail, was special. He had been given to Pinky when he was a baby, and Pinky loved him best.

In her room in the house across the street, Rex said goodbye to her friends, too. She had some bears and cats and even a pig, but she didn't love them best. Her special friends were her dinosaurs. She knew all their names and how to spell them (even the pterodactyl). In fact, Rex knew just about everything you might think there is to know about dinosaurs. And she loved them all. Each and every one.

After she had eaten her breakfast, Rex ran outside and across the street to Pinky's house.

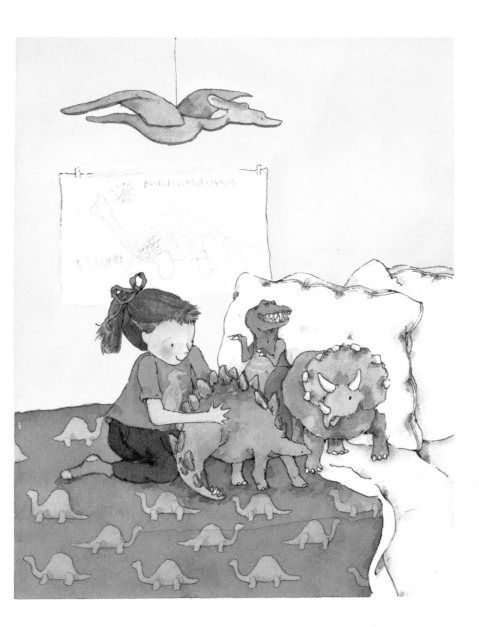

"Pinky has twenty-seven animals," Amanda told her when she came to the door. "I counted."

"Really?" Rex said. "I have twenty-seven dinosaurs."

"That's too many," Amanda said. "You should give me some."

"Let's go!" Pinky's father
shouted, and everyone ran to the car.
Amanda climbed into the front
seat next to her father. Pinky and Rex
got into the backseat. "Does she
have to go with us?" Rex whispered.
Pinky gave her a look, as if to say,
"What can I do?"

15

Sometimes Pinky wished he was an only child like Rex. It was not easy having Amanda tag along on their friendship. He closed his eyes and hoped that Amanda would be gone when he opened them.

But then he felt Rex's fingers tickling him. He tickled her back. Soon he forgot all about Amanda, who was busy in the front seat counting the number of bug spots on the windshield.

"I'm glad I have twenty-seven dinosaurs and you have twenty-seven animals," Rex told Pinky when they stopped their tickling. "That way we have everything the same!"

Pinky nodded his head. "We have to have everything the same," he said. "We're best friends."

Chapter 3
At the Museum

The museum was a very big place full of interesting things to see. Pinky and Rex had been there many times. They knew just where the dinosaur room was, and they always saved it until the end.

"How much time do we have?" Pinky asked his father.

"We have about two hours," his father said. "Then we'll go home for lunch. Where shall we begin?"

"Dinosaurs!" Amanda cried. Pinky and Rex looked at each other. Amanda didn't know how to save the best until last.

Pinky's father understood how Pinky and Rex felt about the dinosaur room. "Why don't we see something else first?" he said. "There's a new American Indian display. I read about it in the newspaper. Amanda, I'll bet you have never seen such a long canoe."

"I have never seen a canoe at all," said Amanda. "I don't even know what a canoe is. I want to see the dinosaurs."

"I know you do," said her father. "But first, let's take a look at this canoe."

"Good idea," said Pinky.

"Great idea," said Rex.

Amanda didn't say anything. She just scrunched up her face and crossed her arms.

20

Pinky and Rex agreed with
Pinky's father that the canoe was the

longest they had ever seen. Amanda
said it was just a boat and who cares?

Next, they saw the wild animals of North America and decided the bobcat was their favorite. Amanda said, "Who cares? They're all dead, anyway."

After that, they went to look at the minerals and ores. Rex thought the emeralds were prettiest. Pinky liked the quartz crystals. Amanda said, "They're only rocks. Who cares?"

Finally, after stopping every few minutes so Amanda could go to the bathroom or get a drink of water or pick something off the bottom of her shoe, they came to the dinosaur room.

"At last!" Rex said. "Now maybe she'll stop being such a grump!"

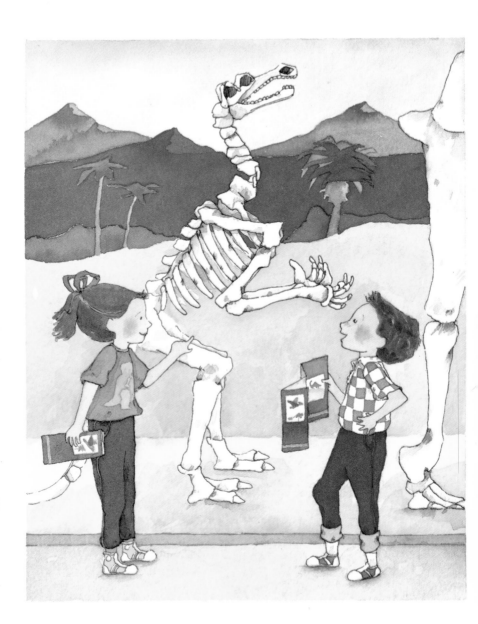

"Look, Amanda," said Pinky.
"Here are the dinosaurs."

"I'm hungry," said Amanda. "I
want to go home."

Pinky and Rex looked up at
Pinky's father. "Why don't Amanda
and I rest on this bench while you
look at the dinosaurs?" he said.
"Then we'll stop at the gift shop and
go home."

Rex grabbed Pinky's hand and
off they went. The last thing they
heard was Amanda saying, "Who
cares about a bunch of bones?"

Chapter 4
Amanda to the Rescue

Rex loved the gift shop. There were so many dinosaur things to buy. The problem was that she had them all. She had every dinosaur T-shirt, and every dinosaur glass, and every dinosaur pencil and pin and poster.

Pinky loved the gift shop, too. He always liked to see what new

animals they had. This time, he saw
that there were some new bears and
tigers and elephants. But he already
had a bear and a tiger and an elephant.
Besides, they cost more money
than he had to spend. And they
didn't have a speck of pink on them
anywhere.

Amanda stood in the middle of the store, with her arms crossed. "I want something," she said. "But I don't know *what!*"

All at once, Pinky looked up and saw just what it was he wanted. It was pink, and it was a kind of animal he didn't have.

At the same moment, Rex saw what she wanted to buy. It was a kind of dinosaur she did not have in her collection. She had never seen one like it before.

Amanda saw what *she* wanted, too. She ran for it. She reached for it. And she felt two other hands on hers.

Pinky and Rex and Amanda all wanted the same thing.

"I *have* to have this dinosaur," Rex said. "I don't have one like it."

"But it's *pink*," said Pinky. "What do you want with a pink dinosaur? *I* have to have it, because it's pink and it's an animal I don't have already."

"You have *too* many animals, Pinky," said Amanda. "And Rex has too many dinosaurs. *I* should have it."

They made such a noise that Pinky's father came over with someone who worked in the store. "I'm afraid that is the last one we have," said the salesclerk.

"How much is it?" Pinky asked, digging into his pocket. He did not let go of the dinosaur.

"Three dollars and fifty cents," the salesclerk said.

Pinky's face fell. "I have *one* dollar and fifty cents," he said.

"Me, too," said Rex. She let go of the dinosaur. So did Pinky. Amanda looked surprised to find that she was holding it all by herself.

"I didn't want it, anyway," Rex said. "If I bought it, then I'd have twenty-eight dinosaurs and you'd have only twenty-seven animals."

"I know," said Pinky. "And if I bought it, I'd have twenty-eight animals and you'd have only twenty-seven dinosaurs. I didn't want it, either."

"Then *I* will buy it," said Amanda.

"Wait a minute!" Rex cried. "I have an idea, Pinky. Let's put our

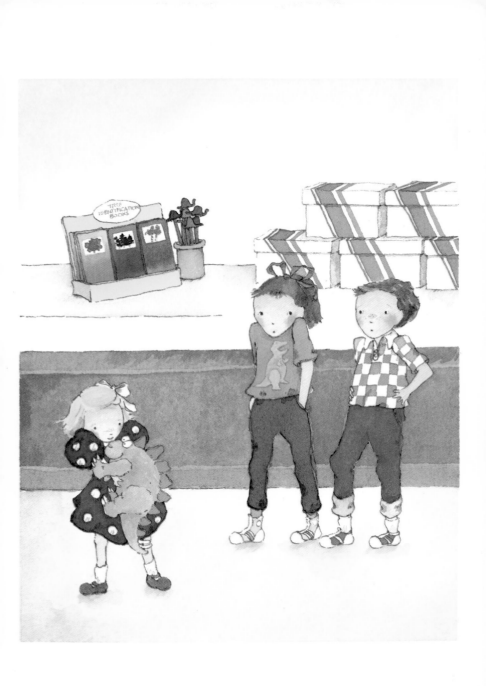

money together and share it. You can keep it half the week, and I'll keep it the other half."

"And then we'll still have everything the same! Good thinking," said Pinky. They yanked the dinosaur out of Amanda's hands and ran to pay for it.

"What about *me*?" Amanda yelled.

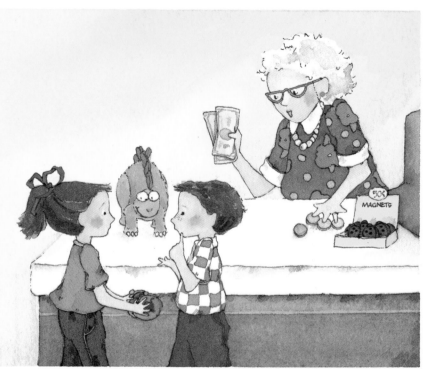

Pinky and Rex put all their
money out on the counter.

"You have only three dollars,"
said the salesclerk. "You need fifty
cents more."

"*I* have fifty cents," they heard
someone say.

37

Pinky and Rex turned around. Amanda had two quarters in her hand and a big smile on her face.

"Sold!" said the clerk.

And so on Mondays and Tuesdays and Wednesdays, the pink dinosaur lives in Rex's room with all her other dinosaurs. And on Thursdays and Fridays and Saturdays, the pink dinosaur lives in Pinky's room with all his other animals.

And each and every Sunday, the pink dinosaur lives in Amanda's room—with Amanda.